Take a Stand!

EVERYTHING YOU NEVER WANTED TO KNOW ABOUT GOVERNMENT

Written by Daniel Weizmann

Illustrated by Jack Keely

PRICE STERN SLOAN

Los Angeles

Editor: Lisa Rojany
Assistant Editor: Kristin Harpster
Art Director: Sheena Needham
Book Designer: Ellen Laning

Library of Congress Cataloging-in-Publication Data

Weizmann, Daniel, 1967–
    Take a stand! / by Daniel Weizmann.
       p.   cm.
    Includes bibliographical references and index.
    Summary: Describes how the United States government works, and how to get involved in politics including school elections, letter-writing campaigns, and mock political debates.

ISBN 0-8431-7997-X

    1. United States—Politics and government—Juvenile literature.
    2. Civics—Juvenile literature.
    3. Student government—United States—Juvenile literature.
    4. Students—United States—Political activity—Juvenile literature.
      [1. United States—Politics and government. 2. Civics. 3. Student government.
      4. Citizenship.]

I. Title.
JIK40.W35 1996   320.473—dc20   96-1117   CIP   AC

First Edition
1 3 5 7 9 10 8 6 4 2

PRICE STERN SLOAN
Los Angeles

When Christopher Columbus first set sail across the Atlantic Ocean way **back in 1492** on strict orders from the Queen of Spain, he had no idea that he was beginning the most important experiment in government in the history of the human race.

In the late 1700s, almost three hundred years later, the American colonies were firmly established in North America, and they wanted their **freedom.** Not just freedom from England, King George III, and unfair taxes, but real lasting freedom—freedom from all kings, all unfair rules, and all unfair rulers.

Early in the morning of April 19, 1775, Paul Revere rode out to warn the countryside that King George III had sent troops to arrest colonial leaders John Hancock and Samuel Adams. A group of armed minutemen greeted the British soldiers, and so began the War for Independence. We had taken our first stand.

On July 2, 1776, the **Continental Congress** took a vote and accepted the resolution that "The United Colonies are, and right ought to be, free and independent States." Two days later, the **Declaration of Independence**, written mostly by Thomas Jefferson, was formally adopted. The next year, the Second Continental Congress adopted the **Articles of Confederation**— a document that called for a loose group of separate states without any central government. The Articles of Confederation worked fine during the war with England. But when the war came to an end, the various states began to quarrel and fight among themselves! The **Founding Forefathers** of our nation—George Washington, Benjamin Franklin, James Madison, Alexander Hamilton, and others— decided to draw up a new document that would be stronger and more effective than the Articles of Confederation.

This new document was the **Constitution of the United States**, and it is still our single most important collection of rules. As our forebears wrote this Constitution, they were determined to establish a new kind of government, where the people could help decide how their lives should be run—in other words, a democracy.

What Is Democracy?

Simply put, democracy is government by the people.

Democracy comes from the Greek words *Demos* (the people) and *Kratia* (authority). The Greeks granted authority to the people. They used these words to mean government by the many, instead of government by a select few or a single king.

In those days democracy was direct. In Athens and other Greek city-states, all the free citizens would gather to discuss and pass laws. They didn't have senators and representatives the way we do today in the United States.

Today's democracy is a little more difficult to understand. Even for many adults, the subject of democracy and government is a confusing one. For one, today's democracy is **representative** rather than direct. We elect people who represent our interests and who help us pass the laws. There's simply too many of us to gather in the town square and vote by raising our hands! Still, no matter how you slice it, democracy is government by the people. And that includes

YOU!

Ask an Expert: Yourself!

- What aspects of your day are "democratic"?

- When do you get to decide what to do, and when are things decided for you?

- Which do you prefer?

The History of Democracy

In the days before government, people had to fight to survive. They hunted wild animals and battled rival tribes. Back then, the strongest fighters and eldest survivors were the leaders and decision-makers.

The Greeks started the voting system about 2,500 years ago. They would often gather in the town square and vote by raising their hands. Sometimes they selected black or white pebbles to show their choices. The Romans kept up this tradition, often using it to decide law cases. Although this is where democracy began, only select people were allowed to vote. In ancient Greece and Rome, many slaves and other people were considered noncitizens without rights.

For most of the next two thousand years, the world was ruled by kings and queens—people who got their position of power by birth or by war. Kings and queens had the ultimate say: Nobody could defy their word or stop them from passing a law. It was a tough way to live because the kings and queens didn't always have your best interests in mind when they made decisions!

Finally, during the 1700s, people began to rebel against their leaders. The American colonists rebelled against King George III, who ruled the colonies all the way from England! When George III sent in troops to collect taxes and arrest rebels, the colonists fought back. Once the king had been conquered, the newly free people debated

on how to create a better system. They chose democracy, so they could have a fair shot at deciding what happened in their communities.

The truth is, it wasn't all that fair at first. Poor people couldn't vote. African Americans and Native Americans couldn't vote. And women couldn't vote. The only people who could vote were wealthy white men.

One by one, each group fought hard to win their right to participate in the democracy. Today, every citizen of the United States who is eighteen years or older can vote. And if you're under eighteen there are still hundreds of ways to participate in government, including holding mock elections, volunteering, and participating in school elections.

Sadly, today many people who have the right to vote either do not understand how to vote, or do not care enough to cast their ballot. These people are letting others make important decisions for them! That's like asking a stranger to pick out your clothes for you!

Don't let this happen to you! We encourage you to take the time to understand your government and participate in every way you can. That way, when you turn eighteen, you won't be afraid to help run the country. It truly is your government. Without you there would be no nation to run!

Why Democracy Is Cool

Democracy is based on three basic principles:

- Every **individual** person is part of government. When laws are passed, they should serve the individual. In the old days, if a ruler wanted a library on the west side of town, that's where it would be built, even if all the people lived on the east side. The system didn't serve individuals.

- Each individual person is **equal**. This doesn't mean that every person can play basketball or solve math problems as well as the next person. It means that the rights and needs of one person are as important as those of any other person.

- Every equal individual wants **freedom**. Freedom is the ability to make choices and to act on them. Let's say you want to run for student body president. If we lived in a society ruled by royalty, you'd have to ask the king's permission to run. Today, you have the freedom to consider whether or not you want to run. You might win, you might not. What's important is that you have the freedom to try.

No man is good enough to govern another man without that other's consent.

READ ALL ABOUT IT!

- **1001 Things Everyone Should Know About American History,** *by John A. Garraty* **(Main Street Books)**

- **Politics: The Basics,** *by Stephen D. Tansey* **(Routledge)**

- **How the U.S. Government Works,** *by Nancy Gendron Hoffman* **(Ziff-Davis Press)**

How
Government
Works

Government

is a little like those Russian matrouchka dolls in which one doll fits inside a bigger doll which fits inside an even bigger one, and so on.

It all starts with you.

You, the citizen, has needs and wants. You require everything from a school, a park, a library, roads, and traffic lights, to a justice system and a military to protect you. It takes a lot of different government systems, big and small, all interconnected, to manage all those needs and wants.

You are a member of your community which is a part of your city.

Your city is run by **local government.** Local government manages the police department, the fire department, the libraries, transportation, and the local courts. The **mayor** heads the city government from **city hall.**

The combined city and county governments are managed by **state government.** State government handles education, public safety, recreation, welfare, and conservation. State government also regulates businesses. The state government is headed by a **governor**, who works in the **state capitol.**

The voters in each of the fifty states elect various members of **Congress.** These senators and representatives meet in Washington, D.C. to manage the affairs of all the combined states in the **federal government.**

The federal government makes decisions that affect all the citizens in the United States. The federal government collects taxes, declares war and regulates the military, makes dollars and coins, and passes laws that are nationwide.

But it doesn't stop there. The federal government of the United States of America is part of a larger worldwide organization: The **United Nations.**

That's a lot of governments! Still, never forget that no matter how large the government may seem, no matter how crowded a chunk of the world it may be managing, the central element of every government is you and citizens just like you.

United Nations

Federal Government

State Government

City Government

Your Community

You!

Ask an Expert: Yourself!

- Do you know where your city hall is located? Your state capitol building?

- Have you ever been affected by decisions made by your community leaders, your local government, your state government, or the federal government?

- What needs or wants do you and your community have that are different from the whole nation's?

- What needs or wants do you and your community share with the whole nation?

World Government

- The United Nations, or UN for short, was formed in 1945 following World War II, to establish and promote world peace and international communication.

- The United Nations building, located in New York City, is a special "international zone," where members of all nations can meet on equal ground to talk. This international zone has its own flag, post office, stamps, and security.

- Originally, only fifty countries agreed to be a part of the United Nations. Today 184 countries belong to the UN—almost the whole world!

The Six Languages of the United Nations are:

Arabic
Chinese
English
French
Russian
Spanish

PREAMBLE TO THE UNITED NATIONS CHARTER

We, the peoples of the United Nations, determined

to save succeeding generations from the scourge of war, which twice in our lifetime has brought untold sorrow to mankind, and to reaffirm faith in fundamental rights, in the dignity and worth of the human person, in the equal rights of men and women and of large and small, and to establish conditions under which justice and respect for the obligations arising from treaties and other sources of international law can be maintained, and to promote social progress and better standards of life in larger freedom.

And for these ends

to practice tolerance and live together in peace with one another as good neighbors, and to unite our strength to maintain international peace and security and to ensure, by the acceptance of principles and the institution of methods, that armed force shall not be used, save in the common interest, and to employ international machinery for the promotion of the economic and social advancement of all peoples.

The United Nations manages world affairs through six main departments:

- The **General Assembly** addresses any important world problem. The General Assembly also appoints the secretary-general who leads the UN and decides the UN's budget.

- The **Security Council** discusses questions of peace and security. Sometimes the Security Council prevents or stops war by having countries talk over their problems and write up a **treaty**. (See *Treaties*, p. 8)

- The **International Court of Justice**, or **World Court**, settles legal disputes between countries. When two countries have a disagreement, they send representatives to this World Court, located in The Hague, a city in the Netherlands. Both countries must vow to obey the decision of the World Court judges.

- The **Secretariat** is the UN staff that handles the daily affairs of the UN.

- The **Economic and Social Council** works closely with organizations such as UNICEF (United Nations International Children's Fund) and WHO (World Health Organization) to solve world problems relating to children, hunger, education, health, and human rights. There are hundreds of opportunities for young people to help these organizations! (See *How You Can Get Involved*, pp.32–42)

- The **Trusteeship Council** watches over the people living in UN territories.

If you would like to get more information about the United Nations, write to:

Public Inquiries Unit Room GA-57, United Nations, New York, NY 10017

"The World State"

Treaties

What happens when two nations want to end a war or disagreement? **Diplomats** from the two nations will get together and write a treaty. Diplomats are specially trained and appointed officials who are skilled in dealing with other countries. The treaty is like a contract that both parties sign and agree to follow.

One of the earliest U.S. treaties was the Treaty of Paris in 1763. After seven years of war, France returned land east of the Mississippi River and south of the Great Lakes. As historian Francis Parkman put it, "Half the continent changed hands at the scratch of a pen."

Have you ever had a disagreement with someone that could have been solved by meeting with them, agreeing on certain terms, and signing a simple contract to make it official?

Government in Space

Ever wonder who will make the rules for outer space? In 1958, the United States formed **NASA** (National Aeronautics and Space Administration) for "peaceful and scientific purposes." On April 12, 1961, Soviet cosmonaut Yuri Gagarin became the first human to orbit Earth. Three weeks later, U.S. astronaut Alan B. Shepard, Jr., of the Mercury 3 mission, became the first American in space. For the next twenty years, during the "Space Race," the United States and Russia were in stiff competition to explore the galaxy.

On February 6, 1995, the U.S. shuttle *Discovery* came within forty feet of the orbiting Russian *Mir* station. Later that year, an American astronaut traveled in a Russian spacecraft and joined cosmonauts on the Mir station. So far, everybody's been happy to cooperate!

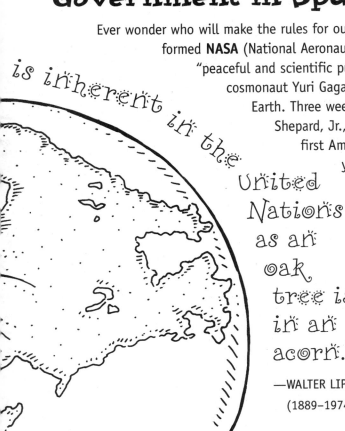

is inherent in the United Nations as an oak tree is in an acorn."

—WALTER LIPPMAN

(1889–1974)

Federal Government

When our forebears got together to start the first modern government, they knew they'd need a signed document to keep the democracy in effect.

Our current government plan was first established at the **Constitutional Convention** in 1787. It didn't actually go into effect until 1789. After several stall-outs and false starts, the main leaders of the day got together in Philadelphia to write the Constitution of the United States. Some of the members present were George Washington, Benjamin Franklin, James Madison, and Alexander Hamilton.

The Constitution is our most important, basic rule book for our government. It establishes a **Bill of Rights** that had been fought for decades.

> The basis of our political system is the right of people to make and alter their constitutions of government.

The Preamble,

an introductory statement to the Constitution, is a declaration that our government was established *by the people*:

"We the people of the United States, in order to form a more perfect Union, establish justice, insure domestic tranquillity, provide for the common defense, promote the general welfare, and secure the blessings of liberty to ourselves and our posterity do ordain and establish this Constitution for the United States of America."

Does your school government have a preamble? Try writing one that will represent the needs and goals of your school government. Here's an example:

"We the students of Mayberry High,

in order to form a more perfect student body, establish school dances, ensure cafeteria tranquillity, collect funds for the yearly fair, promote the daily fun-ness, and secure the blessings of liberty to ourselves and our fellow pupils do ordain and establish this constitution for Mayberry High School."

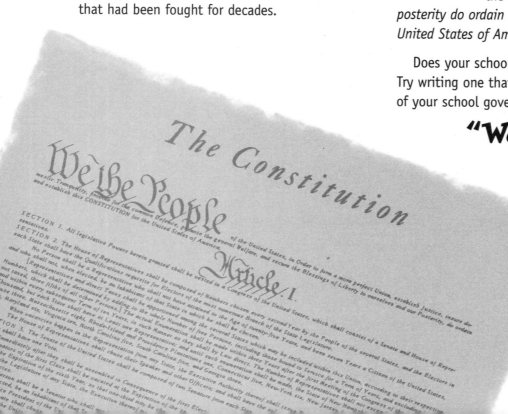

The Bill of Rights: The First 10 Amendments

When we want to add or change laws we create **amendments** to the Constitution. Any amendment must be approved by two-thirds of Congress—the **senators** and **representatives** sent to Washington, D.C., to vote for each state. An amendment must then be approved by three-fourths of all the states (thirty-eight states). The Constitution has only been amended twenty-seven times in the last two hundred years!

The first ten amendments were put into effect in 1791, and are known as the Bill of Rights.

Amendment #1:

Guarantees freedom of religion, speech, and the press. Because our forefathers were *persecuted*—harassed, beaten up, and held back—for their beliefs under King George III of England, they wanted to ensure that we would be free to speak our minds. This is a controversial amendment that is often debated. Should people be allowed to say *anything* they want, even if it hurts others' feelings or isn't completely true? Our forebears said, "Yes."

Amendment #2:

Guarantees the right of the people to have firearms, or weapons for war. Of course, there are many laws that regulate the way that people can *use* firearms.

Amendment #3:

Guarantees that soldiers cannot force their way into your home for a stay. Sometimes, during wartime, traveling soldiers would need emergency hideouts and battle posts. This amendment guarantees that they can't just kick down your door! They need your permission to come in!

Amendment #4:

Protects citizens against being searched or having their property searched or taken away by the government without a good reason.

Amendment #5:

Protects the rights of people on trial for crimes. When people say "I take the fifth!" that means that they are exercising their Fifth Amendment privilege to remain silent in court. This way they don't risk saying something that could land them in jail.

Amendment #6:

Guarantees people accused of crimes the right to a speedy public trial by jury. You can't just hold a suspect and wait a few years to prosecute them. They might be innocent.

Amendment #7:

Guarantees people the right to a trial by jury for cases that aren't criminal.

Amendment #8:

Prohibits cruel and unusual punishments. This does not include homework!

There's More

Amendment #9:

States that specific rights listed in the Constitution do not take away rights that may not be listed. In other words, the Constitution is part of our law, not higher than it.

Amendment #10:

Establishes that powers not granted specifically to the federal government are reserved either for state governments or the people. In a country as large as ours, the federal government can only take care of large problems that affect a majority of the people. Amendment #10 states that if the federal government isn't able to take care of certain local problems, you have the right to gather democratically and take care of them yourselves!

Here are some other important amendments we've made to our Constitution:

1865 — Amendment #13:

Abolished slavery in the United States.

1870 — Amendment #15:

Guarantees that no person, regardless of race or color, can be denied the right to vote.

1920 — Amendment #19:

Grants women the right to vote.

1951 — Amendment #22:

Limits the president to two four-year terms of office.

1971 — Amendment #26:

Lowers the voting age from twenty-one to eighteen.

As you can see, many people had to fight long, hard battles to get truly fair and equal rights. Women didn't have the right to vote until 1920! Even today, many groups struggle for fair treatment in school, at work, and in the community.

Three-Branch Government And the Separation of Powers

The Constitution also introduces a system of **separation of powers** in which three branches of government can check and balance each other. Our three branches of government are the **executive branch** (which includes the president), the **legislative branch** (which includes Congress), and the **judicial branch** (which includes the **Supreme Court**). Each perform separate functions, and check each other's functions in different ways—kind of like a football team where it's one person's job to pass, one person's job to block, and one person's job to run with the ball. Everybody must do their job correctly to achieve the final goal.

CHECKS & BALANCES

Look at how every branch of government is closely watched by another branch of government.

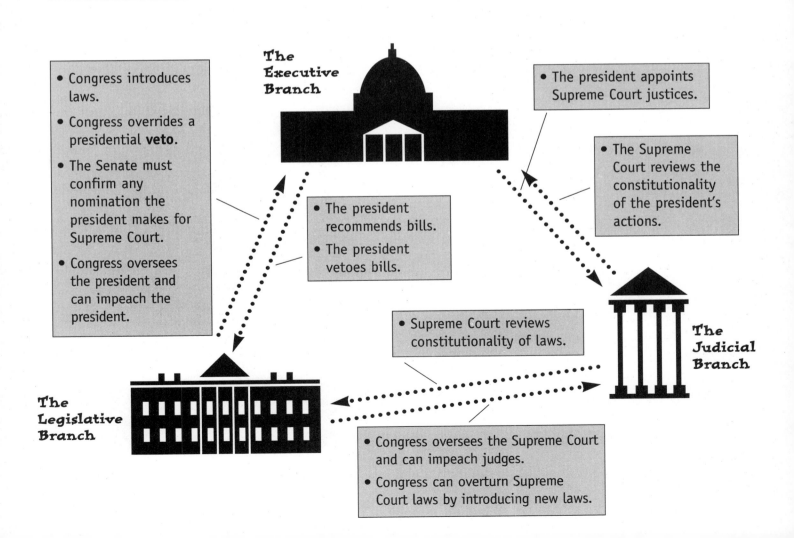

The Executive Branch

- Congress introduces laws.
- Congress overrides a presidential **veto**.
- The Senate must confirm any nomination the president makes for Supreme Court.
- Congress oversees the president and can impeach the president.

- The president appoints Supreme Court justices.

- The Supreme Court reviews the constitutionality of the president's actions.

- The president recommends bills.
- The president vetoes bills.

- Supreme Court reviews constitutionality of laws.

The Judicial Branch

The Legislative Branch

- Congress oversees the Supreme Court and can impeach judges.
- Congress can overturn Supreme Court laws by introducing new laws.

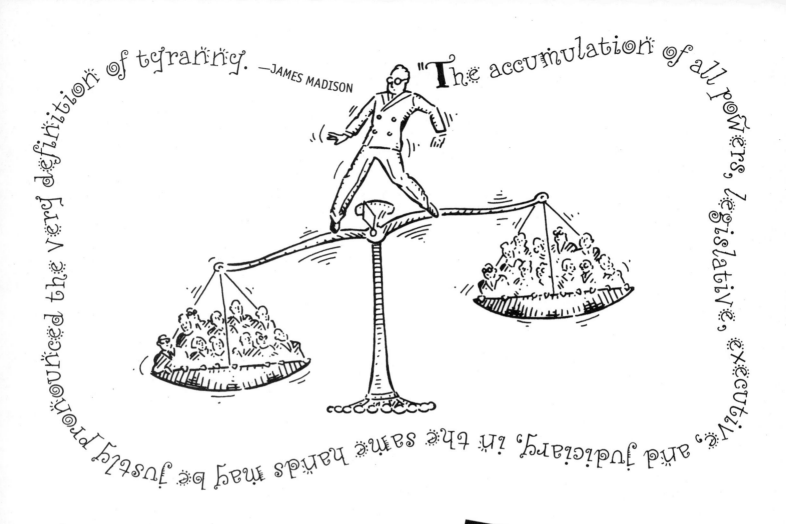

"The accumulation of all powers, legislative, executive, and judiciary, in the same hands may be justly pronounced the very definition of tyranny. —JAMES MADISON

Keeping Your Government in Check

With our special system of **checks and balances**, no one group can gain complete power in the government. By triple-checking everything, government is more likely to represent the needs of more people. If the president (executive office) wants to do something, he or she needs to get the approval of Congress (legislative office), and it can only be done if whatever the president wants to do is constitutional and lawful (judicial office).

But the three branches aren't the only checks and balances in government; the general public as well as private businesses check these three groups. If enough of the voting public isn't satisfied with the way an office is handling things, you can bet that its members and leaders won't get reelected!

Ask an Expert: Yourself!

- Why are checks and balances so important to democracy—government by the people?

- What kind of checks and balances does your student government have?

- How do students keep any one person or group from making all the decisions for them?

The Executive Branch

The executive branch of the federal government includes the president of the United States, the vice president, and the major departments of the government, including:

- State
- Treasury
- Defense
- Justice
- Interior
- Agriculture
- Commerce
- Labor
- Health and Human Services
- Housing and Urban Development
- Transportation
- Energy
- Education
- Veteran's Affairs

Each of these departments have a leader, appointed by the president. The only requirement to be the leader is that you are neither in the **Senate** nor in the **House of Representatives**. Together, all the leaders, along with the vice president and a few other important people, make up the **cabinet**. When the president needs advice, he calls together the cabinet.

Being president of the United States is full-time job! These are just a few of the president's hundreds of responsibilities:

- The president is responsible for enforcing the laws passed by Congress.

- The president is commander in chief of all U.S. armed forces. The president may enter treaties and commit U.S. troops abroad. The president may also declare war.

- The president appoints Supreme Court justices and other federal judges.

- The president recommends **legislation**. The president may also veto legislation that has been passed by the House and the Senate.

- The president tosses the first ball of baseball season!

WANNA BE PRESIDENT? Get in Line!

- If the president is unable to fulfill his or her duties, the vice president must take over. If the vice president cannot fulfill those duties, the Speaker of the House takes over. So far, a Speaker of the House has never become president.

- Fourteen times in American history, the vice president has become a president! John Adams, Thomas Jefferson, Martin Van Buren, John Tyler, Millard Fillmore, Andrew Johnson, Chester Arthur, Teddy Roosevelt, Calvin Coolidge, Harry Truman, Richard Nixon, Lyndon Johnson, Gerald Ford, and George Bush were all vice presidents who went on to become the president!

Close Call!

Don't count your chickens before they hatch! In 1948, the Chicago Tribune jumped the gun and printed the headline Dewey Defeats Truman! *Much to their embarrassment, the vote came in and the rest is history! Truman beat Dewey for the second time in a row!*

How the President Becomes the President

Most U.S. presidents enter the White House after many years of public service. Some have served as state governor or U.S. senator.

To attain the presidency a person has to run two races and win them both: First you need to be nominated at your party's national convention. Then you need to get a majority of the nation's electoral votes on election day.

Finally, after the president has been elected, he or she is sworn into office on January 20 for a four-year term. At the presidential inauguration, the president states "The presidential oath of office."

"I do solemnly swear that I will faithfully execute the office of President of the United States, and will, to the best of my ability, preserve, protect, and defend the Constitution of the United States."

The Electorate

Although the votes of the people are cast on **election day**, the Tuesday following the first Monday in November, the president isn't officially elected until one month later, in December, when the **electoral college** votes. When you vote for a particular candidate, you're really voting for the **elector** who has promised to represent that candidate in December!

There are 538 electors in the electoral college. Each state is allotted one electoral vote per senator and one vote per representative. There are 435 to cover the House of Representatives, 100 for the Senate, and 3 for the District of Columbia. These electors are nominated by political parties. An elector may not be a member of Congress or hold any other federal office.

A candidate must receive 270 electoral votes to win. If no candidate receives 270 votes, the House of Representatives appoints the president. Once, in the 1888 presidential election, Grover Cleveland received more popular votes—votes from the people—than Benjamin Harrison, but Harrison received more electoral votes and went on to become president! Not about to be kicked to the curb, Grover Cleveland came right back and won the next election in 1893!

So You Wanna Be the President?

To run for president of the United States you must be at least thirty-five years old and you must be a native-born citizen and resident of the United States.

Although there have been no female presidents or presidents who are minorities, there are no constitutional laws preventing their election. John Fitzgerald Kennedy was our first-ever Catholic president. You can never be sure who will appeal to the American people next!

42 Fun Facts About 42 Presidents

George Washington

Federalist Party
Served 1789–1797

- When George Washington became president at the age of fifty-seven, he only had one tooth left! Contrary to popular belief, however, he did not have wooden dentures. Washington's false teeth were made out of elephant and walrus tusk.

John Adams

Federalist Party
Served 1797–1801

- John Adams is the only president whose son (John Quincy Adams) also became president!

Thomas Jefferson

Democratic–Republican Party
Served 1801–1809

- When Thomas Jefferson wrote his own epitaph—the inscription on his tombstone—he noted that he was the author of the Declaration of Independence, but he forgot to mention that he had been president of the United States!

James Madison

Democratic-Republican Party
Served 1809–1817

- James Madison, at five feet and four inches tall and only one hundred pounds, was the smallest president. His wife Dolley was one of the most successful first ladies, although she is rumored to have taken snuff, and to have stolen a painting of George Washington from the White House!

John Quincy Adams

Democratic-Republican Party
Served 1825–1829

- As a representative in Congress, John Quincy Adams was given the nickname "Old Man Eloquent" for his enthusiastic speeches on behalf of freedom. He was also famous for being a skinny-dipper!

Andrew Jackson

Democratic Party
Served 1829–1837

- The Creek Indians who fought General Andrew Jackson at the Battle of Horseshoe Bend referred to him as "Sharp Knife."

There's More

"When I was a boy I was told that anybody could become president. I'm beginning to believe it." —CLARENCE DARROW, LAWYER (1857–1938)

The Cost of Being the Prez

George Washington started as president with a salary of $25,000 per term. Not bad for 1787! Today the president receives $200,000 per year plus $50,000 in expenses. In addition, the president receives $100,000 in untaxable travel and entertainment income per year.

Martin Van Buren

Democratic Party
Served 1837–1831

- Van Buren was the first president who was actually born an American citizen. The previous presidents were all born as British subjects.

William H. Harrison

Whig Party
Served 1841

- William Henry Harrison only served thirty-two days—the shortest term of any president. (He died unexpectedly.)

John Tyler

Whig Party
Served 1841–1845

- Because Tyler became president following Harrison's death in office, he was referred to as "His Accidency"! People were unsure whether Tyler really had the authority to run the country.

James K. Polk

Democratic Party
Served 1845–1849

- Polk once said, "I am sure I shall be a happier man in my retirement than I have been during the four years I have filled the office...."

Zachary Taylor

Whig Party
Served 1849–1850

- During the Mexican War, Zachary Taylor was known as "Old Rough and Ready." General Winfield Scott was known as "Old Fuss and Feathers." During the Whig nominations for presidential candidates, "Old Rough and Ready" beat "Old Fuss and Feathers"!

Millard Fillmore

Whig Party
Served 1850–1853

- After leaving the presidency, Fillmore ran again and lost, this time as a candidate for the American, or Know-Nothing Party. They were called the Know-Nothing Party because they claimed to know nothing when they were asked about the party's activities.

Franklin Pierce

Democratic Party
Served 1853–1857

- Pierce would not *ever* swear! During his presidential oath, Pierce said "I do solemnly affirm" instead of "I do solemnly swear."

James Buchanan

Democratic Party
1857–1861

- Buchanan was the only president who never married. He did, however, speak to Queen Victoria through the newly completed transatlantic cable—one of the world's first long distance calls!

Abraham Lincoln

Republican Party
Served 1861–1865

- It is recorded that Abraham Lincoln actually dreamed he would be assassinated the night before he was killed.

Andrew Johnson

Republican Party
Served 1865–1869

- Johnson was drunk when he took his oath of office! Still, he had an excuse: He drank to ease the pain of a bout of a disease known as Typhoid Fever.

Ulysses S. Grant

Republican Party
Served 1869–1877

- U.S. Grant was the first of three presidents in a row who were born in Ohio and acted as generals in the Civil War.

Rutherford B. Hayes

Republican Party
Served 1877–1881

- Rutherford B. Hayes was a champion speller. With a first name like Rutherford, he had to be!

James A. Garfield

Republican Party
Served 1881

- James Garfield liked to perform tricks for his cabinet. He could simultaneously write the same sentence in Greek with his right hand and in Latin with his left hand. He was ambidextrously trilingual!

READ ALL ABOUT IT!

- **Ask Me Anything About The Presidents,** *by Louis Phillips* (Avon Camelot)

- **The Presidents: Tidbits & Trivia,** *by Sid Frank* (Hammond Incorporated)

- **Presidential Posters,** *by Peggy Haynes and Judith Burnham* (Frank Shaffer Publications)

A total of eight presidents have died in office. Four were assassinated: Abraham Lincoln, James Garfield, William McKinley, and John Fitzgerald Kennedy. The other four who died in office were William Henry Harrison, Zachary Taylor, Warren G. Harding, and Franklin Delano Roosevelt. When a president dies in office the vice president becomes president. If the vice president cannot become the president the position goes to the Speaker of the House.

Chester A. Arthur

Republican Party
Served 1881–1885

- Chester was called "The Dude President," because he was such a flashy dresser!

Grover Cleveland

Democratic Party
Served 1885–1889

- Unlike George Washington's walrus fangs, Cleveland had to replace his entire jaw when he lost his teeth. While in the White House, Grover Cleveland was given a new jaw made of rubber.

Benjamin Harrison

Republican Party
Served 1889–1893

- Thomas Collier Platt said of Benjamin Harrison: "Outside the White House ... he could be a courtly gentleman. Inside the executive mansion ... he was as glacial as the Siberian stripped of his furs." (That translates into: "He was a terrific guy to go have a hot dog and see a baseball game with, but he was a cold-blooded, mean, and cruel president.")

Grover Cleveland

Democratic Party
Served 1893–1897

- Grover again?! Yes, Grover Cleveland was the only president to serve two non-consecutive terms in the White House.

William McKinley

Republican Party
Served 1897–1901

- William McKinley is the face on the $500 bill. They're no longer being printed, but if you find one they're still good!

Theodore Roosevelt

Republican Party
Served 1901–1909

- Theodore Roosevelt was the youngest president of the United States. He was forty-two years old when he was sworn in.

William H. Taft

Republican party
Served 1909–1913

- Taft was the first president to own an automobile. He was also the largest president— at 6 feet tall and 340 pounds.

Woodrow Wilson

Democratic Party
Served 1913–1921

• Woodrow Wilson didn't have to go to school until he was nine years old. The schools were all closed because of the Civil War!

Warren G. Harding

Republican Party
Served 1921–1933

• Warren Harding loved to play cards, and referred to his own nomination as drawing "a pair of deuces." Once he finally entered the White House, he gambled away a whole set of china by playing poker!

Calvin Coolidge

Republican Party
Served 1923–1929

• Calvin Coolidge is the only president to be born on July 4—our very own Day of Independence! The year was 1872.

Herbert C. Hoover

Republican Party
Served 1929–1933

• Herbert Hoover picked potato bugs, ran a laundry business, and delivered newspapers to put himself through college.

Franklin D. Roosevelt

Democratic Party
1933–1945

• FDR's mother was the first mom to be able to vote for her son. We're pretty sure she did! Still, we can't be entirely sure, because voting ballots are always secret in the United States (see p. 45).

Harry S. Truman

Democratic Party
Served 1945–1953

• Harry Truman read every book in his hometown library before he turned fourteen!

Dwight D. Eisenhower

Republican Party
Served 1953–1961

• Eisenhower, also known as "Ike," was the first president to hold a pilot's license.

John F. Kennedy

Democratic Party
Served 1961–1963

• JFK received a Pulitzer Prize for his book, *Profiles In Courage*.

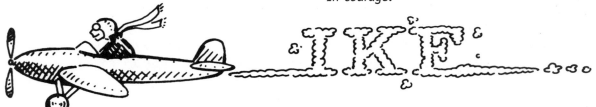

Lyndon B. Johnson

Democratic Party
Served 1963–1969

- LBJ, known for his important role in the Civil Rights movement, was engaged to a daughter of a Ku Klux Klan leader. After Johnson's father criticized the Klan publicly, LBJ called off the engagement.

Richard Nixon

Republican Party
Served 1969–1974

- In 1962, Nixon told reporters, "You won't have Nixon to kick around anymore. Gentlemen, this is my last press conference." Boy was he wrong! Seven years later, he became president.

Gerald Ford

Republican Party
Served 1974–1977

- As a boy, Ford was an Eagle Scout—the highest ranking of Boy Scouts.

James Earl Carter, Jr.

Democratic Party
Served 1977–1981

- Jimmy Carter was a speed-reader who could put down two thousand words a minute! As a busy president, he often read three to four books a week.

Ronald Reagan

Republican Party
Served 1981–1989

- Before becoming president of the nation, Reagan was a radio sports announcer, movie and television actor, president of the Screen Actors Guild, and governor of California.

George Bush

Republican Party
Served 1989–1993

- Bush played first base for Yale University in 1947 and 1948. During his short career, he compiled a .251 batting average in 175 at bats.

William Jefferson Clinton

Democratic Party
Served 1993–?

- Bill Clinton's real name is William Jefferson Blythe III. Before Bill was born, his father died. Four years later, his mother remarried, and he became the legally adopted son of Roger Clinton.

Impeachment

Even the president and the vice president can be kicked out of office, if and only if the House of Representatives "impeaches" them for committing crimes. In 1868, President Andrew Johnson was impeached by the House for defying the Tenure of Office Act but was later found not guilty. In 1974, Republican President Richard Milhous Nixon left the presidential office voluntarily, when a House committee recommended that he be impeached for having stolen information from the Democrats during his campaign.

The Legislative Branch

The legislative branch, also known as the United States Congress, is composed of the Senate and the House of Representatives. Both groups meet in the **Capitol** Building in Washington, D.C.

The chief business of Congress is to study and enact legislation—laws and rules. The Constitution states that Congress collects taxes, borrows money, regulates business, establishes rules for citizenship and bankruptcy, makes dollars and coins, prosecutes counterfeiters, establishes roads and post offices, creates patents and copyrights, establishes small courts, declares war, supports the U.S. Army and the Navy, and governs the District of Columbia (also known as D.C.). Most importantly, the Constitution states that Congress shall "make all laws which shall be necessary and proper for carrying into execution the foregoing powers vested by the Constitution in the government of the United States, or in any department or office thereof."

The two parts of Congress have distinct features:

The House of Representatives

- The House is made up of 435 members. States with the highest population have the most representatives. For instance, California, the most populated state in the union, has 52 representatives. Alaska, Delaware, Montana, North Dakota, South Dakota, Vermont, and Wyoming only have one representative each. When the House of Representatives started out, it only had 65 members!

- Each representative serves for two years.

- Candidates for the House must be at least twenty-five years old and live in the state that they intend to represent.

The Senate

- The Senate is made up of one hundred members, two from each state.

- Each senator serves for six years.

- Every two years, a third of the Senate is newly elected.

- Candidates for the Senate must be at least thirty years old and live in the state that they intend to represent.

Speaker of the House

435 representatives is a pretty big crowd to manage. That's why the Speaker of the House is one of the most important, influential people in U.S. Government. The Speaker of the House addresses representatives on a regular basis, gives or withholds permission to speak, and settles arguments between representatives.

Ask an Expert: Yourself!

- Who are your state's senators and representatives?

- What political parties do they belong to?

- What issues or opinions are they best known for? Have they introduced any bills that have passed?

Party Politics

Since the first political parties developed in the 1790s, the United States has basically been a two-party nation, but those two parties haven't always been the same! The original Democratic party wasn't established until 1828, and the original Republican party wasn't organized until 1854. Both of those parties have gone through many changes before the rise of the primary parties we vote for today. Here are a few of the other parties the U.S. has seen throughout the years.

Federalist Party. George Washington and John Adams are the most famous Federalists. Members of this party supported the U.S. Constitution.

Democratic-Republican Party. Founded in 1792 by Thomas Jefferson, this party opposed the Federalists. Four U.S. presidents were Democratic-Republicans. When this party split in 1828, the Democratic Party was formed.

The Workingmen's Party. Philadelphia union leaders organized this party in 1828. They promoted free public schools and antimonopoly legislation.

The Antimasonic Party. New Yorkers and Pennsylvanians started this party to show their distrust of the Masonic Order (a secret society). In 1831 they organized the first presidential nomination convention.

Whig Party. Originally called National-Republicans, members of this party changed their name to Whigs after the British party that tried to limit the power of the Crown in the 18th century. In America, Whigs opposed the Democratic Party. The Whigs wanted to limit the power held by the executive branch of government.

The Liberty Party. Although its leader, James G. Birney, received 62,000 votes in 1844, this anti-slavery group merged with the Free Soil Party in 1848.

The Free Soil Party. While they did not support abolition of slavery, this party fought to exclude slavery from the territories, and wanted to make it illegal to form new slave states.

The Constitutional Union Party. Ex-senator John Bell from Tennessee won in several states with his platform of trying to keep the North and South at peace. He thought it was important to keep the states together during the Civil War.

Greenback Labor Party. A "green-back" is slang meaning a dollar bill. This party formed during the hard economic times that followed the Civil War. Its members opposed the withdrawal of "greenback" money that was issued during the Civil War.

People's or "Populist" Party. This party wanted a variable income tax (like what we have now), government-owned railroads, and the generation of unlimited silver to increase the supply of money. In 1892, party leader James B. Weaver won more than a million popular votes.

The Progressive Party. Formed in 1912 and headed by Republican Theodore Roosevelt, this original party (two more of the same name were formed in 1924 and 1948) did not want William Howard Taft to run for a second term. Even though Roosevelt received more votes than Taft—over four million—the Republican votes were split between Roosevelt and Taft, and they both lost to Democrat Woodrow Wilson.

Socialist Party. Members of the Socialist Labor Party, who supported the working class, joined this party to support leader Eugene V. Debs. Debs received more than 900,000 presidential votes in 1912.

States' Rights, or "Dixiecrat" Party. Members of this party were conservative Southern Democrats who opposed President Truman.

The Judicial Branch

The Supreme Court consists of nine justices who are appointed by the president for life, or until they decide to retire. There is one chief justice and eight associate justices in the Supreme Court.

The Supreme Court reviews federal and state laws and treaties to make sure that they do not conflict in any way with the U.S. Constitution. If they do conflict, they are declared unconstitutional. This process is called **judicial review**.

"I'll take this case all the way to the Supreme Court!" is the usual cry of an aggressive attorney. Most often, the cases the Supreme Court reviews have been through state and federal trial courts, appellate courts, or United States district courts. Only a couple of hundred cases get to the Supreme Court each year.

Opinion Mondays

If you happen to be in Washington, D.C., and want to visit the U.S. Supreme Court, be sure to pop in on "Judgment Day" also known as "Opinion Monday." Every month for two weeks, the Supreme Court hears cases. They then recess for two weeks to write their opinions. Each Monday at noon, the Court hands down its supreme, incontestable opinion. Once the Supreme Court delivers its verdict, a case cannot be retried.

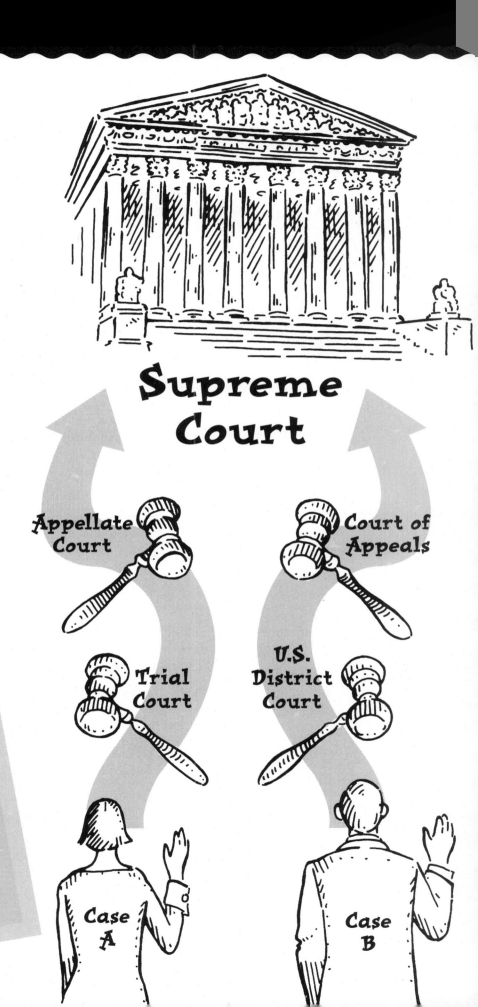

Supreme Court

Appellate Court

Court of Appeals

Trial Court

U.S. District Court

Case A

Case B

Famous Cases of the Supreme Court

- **1819:** *McCulloch v. Maryland.* Congress was given power to establish a national bank that could not be taxed by the states.

  - **1931:** *Near v. Minnesota.* A Minneapolis newspaper printed a story about a known gangster who was bribing the chief of police. By order of a Minnesota court, the paper was prevented from ever being published. However, the editor appealed to the Supreme Court which declared that the press had liberty under the First Amendment to print what they wanted, even if it was going to cause controversy or ruin somebody's reputation.

  - **1937:** In the heart of the Great Depression, when money was scarce, the Supreme Court upheld the Social Security Act, guaranteeing that Congress can tax citizens for the "general welfare of the United States."

  - **1954:** *Brown v. Board of Education of Topeka.* The Supreme Court declares that eleven-year-old African American Linda Brown was unconstitutionally denied access to an all-white school. The Supreme Court declared for the first time that "separate educational facilities are inherently unequal."

- **1961:** *Mapp v. Ohio.* It is determined that evidence obtained without a search warrant is not admissible in court because it violates the Fourth Amendment.

- **1962:** *Engel v. Vitale.* The Supreme Court establishes that requiring students to recite a prayer in public schools violates the First Amendment.

- **1986:** *Ford v. Wainright.* The Court decides that the Constitution forbids giving insane prisoners the death penalty.

Filibuster!

Want to stop a bill from becoming a law in the Senate? Talk it to death! A **filibuster** is a nonstop debate tactic in which a senator will talk and talk and talk about why a bill should be dropped until the other senators give up and give in. This style was made popular in the movie Mr. Smith Goes to Washington, starring Jimmy Stewart as a motor mouth senator!

Just How Do Federal Laws Get Made Anyway?

A proposed law is called a bill.

Let's say (just for fun) that you and your friends wanted to paint all the doors in all the schools bright purple. You need a **bill**.

1. Get Support For Your Bill

First you'd have to organize a big enough group of people to support your proposed bill. You might start by asking everyone you can to sign a petition that demands that all doors in all schools be painted purple. This petition would usually have to have the endorsement of members of city and state government behind it.

2. Get Senators and Representatives To Propose Your Bill

With enough support and signatures, your senator or representative might author the purple door bill. Your senator or representative would then introduce the bill and become the bill's **sponsor**.

3. The Bill Gets Cleaned Up

Legislative counsel would review and clean up the bill, making sure that the request was completely legal and constitutional. If there was already an amendment in the federal Constitution which stated that all school doors were to be painted orange and only orange, it would be a more difficult bill to pass. *The purple door bill will be printed and held for thirty days before its first committee hearing.*

4. The Bill Gets Reviewed

Both the House of Representatives and the Senate will forward the bill to appropriate committees for review. A National Purple School Door Bill might be sent to all the education and labor committees in the House and the Senate. The committees hold hearings where various people can speak for or against the bill. The different committees make small changes to the bill as they see fit and present it to the House and the Senate for debate.

5. The Bill Gets Debated On

The House and the Senate debate separately and change the bill yet again. For example, the House may want the law to reflect that only every other door in every other school be painted purple. The Senate may want all doors painted purple, but only in schools in 25 states. Once they have decided how to amend the bill, they vote on it.

6. The Bill is Held by a Conference Committee

If both the House and the Senate pass different versions of the same bill, the bill must then go to a **conference committee**, to iron out differences. Perhaps the bill will now reflect that every other door should be painted in every other school in every other state.

7. The Final Bill is Voted On

Finally, the House and the Senate vote on this agreed-upon version of the bill. If it passes again, it goes to the president to sign.

8. The President Signs or Doesn't Sign the Bill

The president has the power to VETO! If the president doesn't want to sign the bill, it goes straight back to Congress. This is called "vetoing the bill," and only the president has this power. However, the returned bill can get voted on again by Congress, and if two-thirds of the House and the Senate still pass the bill, knowing that the president has rejected it, it becomes a law. Thus, with a two-thirds vote, Congress can "override" the president's veto.

Take a Stand! Word Search

Can you find the following words right before your very eyes?!

UNITED	NATION	SLOGAN	JUSTICE	BALLOT
GOVERNMENT	PRESIDENT	VICE	VETO	ELECT
FILIBUSTER	CONSTITUTION	FREEDOM	WASHINGTON	VOLUNTEER
REPRESENTATIVE	SENATE	BILL	EXEC	STATE
UNANIMOUS	VOTE	HOUSE	DEMOCRACY	

M	Q	G	O	N	S	A	F	Z	T	X	O	O	Z	W	E	N	D	O
T	E	L	O	K	T	N	O	I	T	U	T	I	T	S	N	O	C	J
J	K	Q	C	V	I	C	E	T	A	T	S	K	H	T	T	J	O	H
Z	O	E	E	O	E	L	V	W	A	S	H	I	N	G	T	O	N	E
O	H	T	L	L	P	R	E	S	I	D	E	N	T	V	O	O	G	R
C	O	X	E	U	G	D	N	B	E	J	B	A	L	L	O	T	R	E
X	U	K	C	N	M	D	E	M	O	C	R	A	C	Y	L	T	E	T
M	S	B	T	T	F	R	O	B	E	C	O	N	L	B	N	L	E	S
O	E	I	S	E	N	A	T	E	O	N	D	O	L	A	M	A	I	U
D	L	L	O	E	G	Y	T	A	E	R	T	I	F	R	N	N	W	B
E	I	L	M	R	E	P	R	E	S	E	N	T	A	T	I	V	E	I
E	C	I	T	S	U	J	C	O	N	G	R	A	A	Q	L	P	X	L
R	D	D	S	L	O	G	A	N	W	D	U	N	I	T	E	D	E	I
F	A	U	N	A	N	I	M	O	U	S	S	E	G	N	N	O	C	F

(Answers on page 64)

Match the Anti People!

Americans are famous for speaking their minds against groups and policies they disagree with. See if you can match these Anti's with their definitions! Answers on p. 64.

—— **1.** Antinomians
—— **2.** Antifederalists
—— **3.** Antimasons
—— **4.** Anti-Imperialist League
—— **5.** Antimonopoly Party
—— **6.** Antibigamy Act
—— **7.** Antitrust Movement
—— **8.** Antisaloon League of America
—— **9.** Anti-Injunction Act
—— **10.** Anti-Anticommunism
—— **11.** Antiballistic Missile Treaty

a. A law that prevents people from having more than one wife or one husband.

b. They were against companies that combined to control competition.

c. This law stopped judges from preventing peaceful picketing.

d. They didn't want the U.S. to acquire the Philippine islands.

e. They didn't believe in communism, but they opposed the harassment of communists!

f. They believed that salvation depended on God's grace.

g. They accused a secret society of killing a bricklayer.

h. A document to limit arms.

i. They had nothing against board games, but they ran a presidential candidate who supported economic reform.

j. They opposed the Constitution and strong central government.

k. They sought the end of alcohol use.

(Answers on page 64)

Long before you turn eighteen and are ready to vote, you can be a part of government and an active member of your community. There are hundreds of opportunities for kids and young adults to help others, help the environment, express opinions on important issues, help candidates they support, and take a stand!

Grassroots Activity

When people organize themselves to improve their community or the world, it is known as **grassroots** activity. One great way for young people to help the world is by forming grassroots groups to take on special tasks. Here are just a few examples of the kinds of grassroots groups you can form with nothing more than a few friends and a lot of energy!

Start a Recycling Center

- Ask a friend to be your **recycling** partner. Make a plan to organize your recycling center together. Always travel with a friend—it'll be safer and you'll have more fun!

- Check your yellow pages under "recycling" for a place that will take your cans, bottles, and newspapers. Find out where the place is located and the hours they are open. Ask them how they like to receive the recyclable goods. They may want the cans bagged or the newspapers tied.

- Ask your neighbors, apartment managers or landlords, and local stores, restaurants, and hotels if they would like to participate in your recycling program.

- Get cardboard boxes and old trash cans from local supermarkets and attach signs that tell people where to leave recyclable goods. Make sure you have separate bins for plastic, glass, paper, and aluminum.

- Make fliers telling the neighborhood where the bins will be located and when you will take the full bins to the recycling place. Make sure that the flyer tells them how important it is to recycle. By saving reusable goods we are saving the planet!

- Sit back and wait for the cans to fill up! Make sure that people put the right stuff in the right cans before you take it to your local recycling place.

Hold a Community Garage Sale

- There's power in numbers! Along with your friends, get your neighbors to participate in a super-sized garage sale. Garage sales are like recycling programs because they get people to reuse things instead of throwing them away.

- Make a pact with your neighbors to donate a portion of the money you receive to a good local cause.

- Take the stuff you don't sell to the local Salvation Army or veterans' center! That way somebody may have a chance to use it before it becomes more garbage.

Political Activism

- During election time, you may want to assist with voter registration. The best way to do this is to look in your telephone book for the local chapter of a political party or voting organization.

- On election day itself, you may want to help voters at your nearest polling place. You can find out where people will be voting by calling your city hall.

- If there is a candidate that you particularly believe in, chances are he or she has a campaign center near you, and can use your help. You may be enlisted to pass out buttons, hang posters, or simply make copies and do odd jobs.

Fundraising

- Is there a cause that you want to support that needs your money? In Ontario, Canada, a school class raised $7,000 to help save over two hundred acres of rain forest.

- If you have something to sell or a special skill to offer, you can raise funds! People tend to be more generous when they know you are selling something for a good cause, especially if you give them a certificate that thanks them for participating.

If you are a good artist, try selling your own holiday cards or framed pictures. You might want to create and sell art from recycled aluminum, plastic, and paper products. You can also put on a show or hold a game and charge for tickets, or provide services such as washing cars or mowing lawns.

Positive Picket!

- Pick four or five local restaurants willing to enter a contest for environmental consciousness.

- Hold a contest to see which restaurant is doing the most to recycle.

- Inspect that restaurant's kitchen and packaging materials—with their permission of course!

- Gather your data and go over it with friends. Decide which restaurant or restaurants are doing the best job for the environment.

- Help the winning restaurants celebrate by marching outside the establishment with positive signs, like THIS RESTAURANT CARES ABOUT THE ENVIRONMENT or BUY FOOD HERE!

Letter Writing Campaigns

Although you may not be old enough to vote, you are always old enough to write government officials and tell them how you feel. If enough people all address the same issue in letters to a particular official, that official is sure to take notice. They want to get reelected, so they are going to do what they can to please their citizens!

You can write almost any government official, but first you must decide which government official is responsible for the issue you are addressing. Don't write to the president about problems in your school cafeteria, and don't write the mayor about the world peace conference at the United Nations because they won't be able to help you with those particular issues!

Chain of Command

One rule of thumb for a letter-writing campaign is following the chain of command. Start with the most accessible official, and work your way up until you get a response you are satisfied with. For school issues such as starting a new club or program, you can write to your principal. If your principal cannot help you, he or she may recommend that you write to the superintendent of the local school board in your county. It's always best to get permission from the official who is closest to you. For local problems, write to the mayor of your city first, then the governor of your state. In addition to the list we have provided here, you may want to check your telephone book to find addresses for officials and the departments they represent.

If the issue you are addressing involves many levels of government, you may want to send the same letter to several officials. The best way to do this is to address the letter to the highest official and *CC:* the others. CC: stands for *carbon copy*. In the days before photocopiers and computers, people used carbon sheets to make copies of the same letter. As illustrated on the next page, just write CC: at the bottom of the letter, followed by the official names of the others to whom you will send the letter. Make copies and send them the same letter at once.

Always write government officials in a proper business format,

with your name and address in the upper right corner, followed by the date. Then, on the left, list the official's formal name and address, address the official and follow with a concise, simple letter.

There are five important elements to a proper official letter. First, explain the issue at hand as briefly as possible; chances are, your representative is familiar with it. Second, clearly state your opinion about the issue. Third, tell the official why you have this opinion and why the outcome affects you personally. Fourth, tell the official exactly what you want them to do. Is there a bill that represents the issue, or an upcoming vote? Can they start or stop an official program to make things better? Be clear about your purpose. Finally, thank the official for their time and explain that you are not old enough to vote but that you will be someday!

Here's an example of a good official letter:

Now you can check the papers to see how your congresspeople vote! Did the mayor vote with you or with the **city council**? When you are old enough, will you help reelect him or her?

Tony Citizen
1212 Maple Lane
Sloanville, Connecticut 33313

January 10, 1999

The Honorable Tanni Fujimoto
Mayor of Sloanville
City Hall
Sloanville, Connecticut 33333

Dear Mayor Fujimoto:

I recently read in the *Sloanville Bee* that the city council is trying to pass a law that forbids people to raise frogs in their bathtubs. I am writing this letter to let you know that I do not think this law should be passed!

While raising a frog in my own bathtub this summer, I learned much about frogs and nature. I don't have a backyard and wouldn't have been able to raise the frog, which I named Frankie, had my mother not allowed the bathtub to be his home. Today, my frog is a fine, upstanding pet who never gets in our way, and I am a good pet owner who knows how to care for an animal.

Please vote against the city council this season when they try to pass this anti-frog-in-the-bathtub law!

Thank you for your time and understanding. Although I am still too young to vote, I plan on being an active voter when I grow up!

Yours Truly,

Tony C.
Tony Citizen

cc: President Clinton
Frankie the Frog

Congratulatory Letters

You don't need to want to fix something or complain about something to write a letter! You can write a letter to congratulate an official on a job well-done! Again, always clearly explain what it is you are pleased with, and let your official know how their decisions or actions personally affect you. Many will be especially pleased to hear that they are doing the right job for kids. They know that you are the voters of tomorrow!

Address the Government

It is always important to properly address government officials. Following is a list of government officials and their proper form of address. In some cases, you'll need to find out the official's name and the zip code of their location. Only write an official when you really have something important to share, whether that's congratulating them on a particular action, or requesting that they pay attention to a matter that directly affects you.

The President

The President
The White House
Washington, D.C. 20500

Dear Mr. (or Ms.) President:
   or
Dear President McDougal:

The Vice President

The Vice President
Old Executive Office Building
Washington, D.C. 20501

Dear Ms. (or Mr.) Vice President:
   or
Dear Vice President Rojany:

U.S. Senator

The Honorable Mahoney
United States Senator
Senate Office Building
Washington, D.C. 20510

Dear Senator Mahoney:

U.S. Representative

The Honorable Hadley
House of Representatives
Rayburn Building
Washington, D.C. 20515

Dear Representative Hadley:

Governor

The Honorable Jean Sund
Governor of Your State
Your State Capitol
Your State Capital City,
State, Zip Code

Dear Governor Sund:

Mayor

The Honorable Tanni Fujimoto
Mayor of Your City
City Hall
Your City, Your State, Zip Code

Dear Mayor Fujimoto:

Please see our very special "Government on the internet" section featuring Web site addresses and information.

PAGE 60.

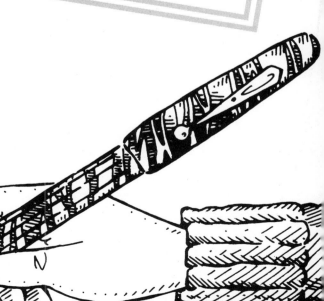

Volunteer!

Volunteering is a fun way to help people and make the world a better place. There are volunteering opportunities for kids in every community in the United States.

What are the concerns of your local community? Is your neighborhood clean and safe? Do the people—all the people—have shelter, clothing, and enough to eat? Are the parks and libraries and other places that everybody shares in good shape?

Save the Globe

One major concern of all communities today is the environment. The environment's got big problems and it's going to take heroic volunteers like you to save it!

We live in what is known as an **ecosystem**. All of nature—from the wildlife to the trees to the oceans to you—is part of this system.

Humans have upset the delicate balance this ecosystem needs to function properly, and it's up to us to fix it while we still can!

***Here's an example of
how things get messed up:***

Let's say we need a whole bunch of paper to make books like the one you're holding right now. We cut down a bunch of trees. No big deal. We've been doing it for years.

What we may not have realized is that those trees provided food and shelter for a certain family of bugs. Bugs who fed on the tree's leaves die off. Once the bugs are gone, the local birds have nothing for lunch. They aren't just going to hang around and get hungry! They go to another forest to look for food. They might not find what they're looking for because Earth has limited resources. In addition, the trees, which held the soil in place are gone so the soil washes away with the rain, ruining the opportunity for new trees to grow.

Most importantly, the trees provide oxygen and filter harmful pollutants, not just for birds and bugs, but for you and me! While we thought we were just removing a few trees to make paper, we were really choking ourselves, and running the local wildlife out of town!

This is only one of the many ways our behavior throws the ecosystem out of whack.

Which of the following items can be recycled? A magazine. A phone book. A six-pack. Plastic utensils. A battery. A G

— Cars, factories, spray cans, and even plastic foam cups and trays give off chemicals that enter our atmosphere, deteriorating the ozone layer that protects us from the sun's super-hot rays.

— Animals, some of which are nearly extinct, are unnecessarily killed so their fur can be sewn into fur coats. Again, these animals play a part in their local ecosystems. When they disappear, the animal neighborhood goes topsy-turvy.

— Crops are covered with pesticides to keep bugs off the fruits and vegetables. Unfortunately, when the crops are watered, the poisons get flushed into the rivers. The fish that live in these rivers get poisoned and die, and the animals that eat the fish go hungry—or get sick, too!

— Petroleum is a natural chemical that comes from decayed plant and animal matter that has been trapped below Earth's surface for millions of years. We use the extracted chemical to heat our homes and run our automobiles. Ironically, petroleum cannot be recycled. When this oil is accidentally spilled or is flushed back into the ocean, many different kinds of animals, from otters to crabs are killed.

ilk bottle. A milk carton. wrap. Cellophane. **ANSWER: ALL OF THE ABOVE.**

From the jungles and forests to the oceans and lakes to the rivers and cities, no part of our planet is untouched by the things we do!

It sounds pretty scary, but don't lose hope! Where there's a problem, there's a solution for a courageous volunteer like you.

People like you all over the world are actively volunteering to help save the environment. They're not just doing the world a favor, they're doing themselves a favor by making this a more livable place for themselves, their children, and their children's children.

There are hundreds of ways you can help the environment. Here are just a few:

1) Collect the Cans, bottles, paper, and glass littered throughout your neighborhood. Also collect the glass, aluminum, and paper that is being unneccesarily thrown away with the regular garbage. By law, your local sanitation department must give you bins with which to recycle these goods. Recycling takes minutes out of each day, but if everybody does it, it'll put years back on the earth!

2) Collect Water! It sounds silly but your bathtub drinks gallons and gallons of water while you're waiting for the water to get hot. Collect that water in a pail and reuse it. Even if it's not good enough to cook with, your plants will love it!

3) Walk There! Every time you walk instead of driving, you do the air around you (and your heart!) a big favor. If you must drive, see if you and your friends can organize a car pool, so that at least the air gets a break!

There's More

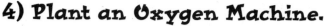

4) Plant an Oxygen Machine.

That is, plant a tree wherever you can. One acre of sycamore trees can filter out fifteen tons of pollution every year!

5) Get a Lunchbox.

Why waste a paper bag and boxes of juice every day when you can keep a neat, clean lunch box and a thermos?

6) Cut the Plastic.

Plastic rings that hold a six-pack of drinks are killers—literally. Sea birds and other animals get caught in the rings and choke to death. Always cut your six-pack holders into tiny bits before recycling the plastic!

7) Pile Up the Paper.

Save, use, and re-use scrap paper. Collect unused portions of paper and leave them by the telephone. Staple slices of scrap paper to a piece of cardboard—and *voilà*! A handy scrap-paper pad. Save newspapers too! If everyone in the United States recycled just one-tenth of their newspapers we could save as many as twenty-five million trees every year. Think of the animal habitats you can save!

8) Hand It Down.

Don't toss old toys, clothes, books, and accessories in the trash! It's a double no-no: You're adding garbage to the planet, and you're depriving somebody who might be able to use what you no longer want! Take all of your hand-me-down clothes and has-been toys to the local Salvation Army or other local giveaway!

9) Flick the Switch to "OFF."

Electric utilities are responsible for 28 percent of the carbon dioxide in our environment. The atmosphere now contains 25 percent more CO_2 than it did a century ago. Scientists predict that the earth will be as much as nine degrees hotter by the year 2050 if we don't cool our electric output. When you can, don't use electricity, gasoline-powered cars, air conditioners, or heaters. Take walks, ride bicycles, skate, and use skateboards to get where you need to go. Wear extra socks and sweaters in the winter, and keep yourself covered with extra blankets at night. In the summer open the windows, and hose yourself down to keep cool!

10) Water the Christmas Tree!

Buy a live Christmas tree and plant it after the holiday season. You'll be giving Planet Earth an extra-special holiday gift!

You can write to any of the conservation organizations listed in our *Get In Touch* section (p. 42) to see what you can do to help the planet!

Human Care

One animal that always needs a helping hand is the human!

A major concern today is human care—care for those who don't have help or can't help themselves, including homeless people, children without families, the frail, the hungry, and the elderly. In your very own community you may see families and individuals who don't have homes to live in or enough food to eat. You probably want to help them, but don't know how. Call your local city hall and ask how you can provide aid to the needy. There are usually a few social service programs which kids can get involved in. Often, these programs give adults, young adults, and children opportunities to help the needy by delivering food, caring for the weak, and even playing with younger children who have only one parent and no brothers or sisters.

Sometimes helping others can be as simple as helping an elderly person or small child cross the street, giving your leftovers to a hungry person, or donating old clothing and toys to a charity instead of throwing them away. Every day we are given chances to help our fellow human beings.

One thing is for sure: If you make an effort to help others, you'll feel good about yourself!

- The United Nations has several programs that you can get involved in. See our *Government on the Internet* section on page 60 for more information about how to contact the United Nations.

- You may also want to call your local city hall and ask how you can get involved in providing aid. Are there people that are starving in your community or town? Many areas have food drives in which people give cans of food for the hungry. If there are no food drives in your area, perhaps you can start one!

Who's Hungry?

Did you ever sit down to a meal and realize how lucky you really are? You may not know how many people really go hungry. The Bread for the World Institute estimates that 205.1 million people did not have enough food in 1970. By 1995, 263.4 million people went hungry. Children under twelve make up 8.8 million of that number. And the number of hungry people increases each year. If we all pitch in a little bit, perhaps we can prevent this statistic from rising by the year 2000.

READ ALL ABOUT IT!

- *Kid Heroes of the Environment,* by The EarthWorks Group (EarthWorks Press)

- *50 Simple Things Kids Can Do to Recycle,* by The EarthWorks Group (EarthWorks Press)

- *50 More Things You Can Do to Save The Earth,* by The EarthWorks Group (Andrews and McMeel)

- *Nickelodeon: The Big Help Book,* by Alan Goodman (Minstrel/Pocket)

- *It's Our World, Too!* by Phillip Hoose (Joy Street/Little Brown)

Get In Touch!

As you can see, there are a number of places you can write to find out more about volunteering, helping the environment, and participating in grassroots activities.

Earth Train
900 North Point
San Francisco, CA 94109

Environmental Youth Alliance
P.O. Box 34097
Station D
Vancouver, B.C. V6J 4M1
Canada

Conservation International
1015 18th Street N.W., Suite 1000
Washington, D.C. 20036

National Wildlife Federation
1400 16th Street N.W.
Washington, D.C. 20036

Caretakers of the Environment
International/USA
2216 Schiller Avenue
Wilmette, IL 60091

Children for Old Growth
P.O. Box 1090
Redway, CA 95560

Nature Conservancy
1815 North Lynn Street
Arlington, VA 22209

Rainforest Action Newsweek
301 Broadway, Suite A
San Francisco, CA 94133

The Wilderness Society
900 17th Street N.W.
Washington, D.C. 20006

Children's Alliance for Protection of the Environment (CAPE)
P.O. Box 307
Austin, TX 78767

Ground Truth Studies Project
The Aspen Global Change Institute
100 East Francis
Aspen, CO 81611

Kids Against Pollution (KAP)
Tenakill School
P.O. Box 775
Closter, NJ 07624

World Conservation Union (IUCN)
1110 Morges
SWITZERLAND

Worldwatch Institute
1776 Massachusetts Avenue, N.W.
Washington, D.C. 20036

Kids for a Clean Environment
(Kids FACE)
P.O. Box 15824
Nashville, TN 37215

Kids for Saving the Earth (KSE)
P.O. Box 47247
Plymouth, MN 55447

World Wildlife Fund
1601 Connecticut Avenue N.W.
Washington, D.C. 20009

World-Wide Fund for Nature
1250 24th Street, N.W.
Washington, D.C. 20037

Kids Network
National Geographic Society
Educational Services
Department 1001
Washington, D.C. 20077

KiDS STOP (Kids Save the Planet!)
P.O. Box 471
Forest Hills, NY 11375

People Educating Other People for a Long-Lasting Environment: Project PEOPLE
P.O. Box 932
Prospect Heights, IL 60070

Student Conservation Association
1800 North Kent Street
Suite 1260
Arlington, VA 22209

Student Environmental Action Coalition (SEAC)
P.O. Box 1168
Chapel Hill, NC 27514-1168

Youth for Environmental Sanity (YES!)
706 Frederick Street
Santa Cruz, CA 95062

How to Hold a Mock Election

One way to help your community is to hold a mock election.

A mock election will help you and and your friends better understand politics, government, and presidential campaigns. And they can be lots of fun!

There are several important steps to holding a successful mock election. First, you'll need to get several friends involved: no less than five and no more than fifteen.

Assign **candidate committees** to represent each presidential candidate.

Each committee needs to research the views of each presidential candidate. This is not always easy! Presidential candidates have been known to contradict themselves.

Good places to search for a presidential candidate's views are:

- Newspaper polls
- Magazine interviews
- Books by or about presidential candidates
- Television interviews
- Television commercials

Each committee should elect their own mock presidential candidate—someone who is a good speaker and who understands what the actual candidate stands for.

The Great Debate

Elect three students to head a **debate committee**. These students will formulate questions to ask each candidate. The debate committee needs to understand the issues as well as the candidate committee does!

Some sample questions might include:

- You have made several promises to the American public. If elected, how do you plan to turn these promises into realities?

- If elected, what do you plan to do about the following issues?
  —Foreign affairs
  —The economy
  —Health care
  —Immigration

- Why is your tax policy better than your opponent's?

- What are you going to do for the schools and students?

- What is your **agenda** for dealing with poverty? The homeless?

Ask candidate #1 a question.

Give candidate #1 five minutes to respond. When the five minutes have passed, let him or her finish a sentence, and say, "Your time is up. Candidate #2, please respond." Give Candidate #2 three minutes to **rebut**—offer opposing arguments and evidence. For the next question, let candidate #2 respond and let candidate #1 rebut. Switch the order for each question.

After each candidate has answered all the questions, it's time to vote! Seal a shoebox shut with tape and cut a one-inch-thick slit down the middle of its lid. This is your **ballot box**, and it needs to be protected.

On three by five inch cards, write the name of each candidate alongside a check box. Pass these cards out to all voters.

Remember that everyone—including the debate team, the candidate teams, and the candidates themselves—gets to vote! On election day, you can bet that the real presidential candidates are going to vote for themselves!

Also, remember that everyone is allowed to vote **anonymously**. In the United States of America, nobody can tell you who to vote for, and nobody can punish you because you voted for a certain candidate. For this reason, and to protect voter privacy, balloting is done in secret.

Assign a time of day by which all voting cards must be in the ballot box. When that time comes, give the ballot box to the debate team to tally. Double-check the count to make sure you know who has been elected. Write the complete results of the vote, including how many people voted for each candidate, on a piece of paper and put it in a sealed envelope for the election officer to announce.

There's More

The only time Zachary Taylor ever took the time to vote for the president of the United States was the time he voted for himself!

Lights! Camera! Debate!

You may want to tape-record or videotape your debate. That way you can review the results and see why one candidate may have made a better impression than the other.

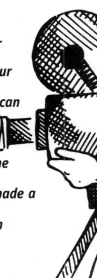

Gather everyone to discuss the results:

- Was it a close call or a landslide? Did each candidate receive about the same amount of votes or did one candidate receive the majority of votes?

- Was the winner your choice? (You're not obligated to tell.)

- Why do you think the winning candidate was elected? What qualities led to their victory?

- What issue or issues were the most important to the election? Did issues decide the winner, or was it some other factor, like personality or popularity?

See how your choices reflect the actual election.

- Did you decide on the same president?

- Does your group of classmates vote similarly or differently in comparison to the country at large? If not, can you guess why?

After the election, follow the news to see which promises or issues the new president follows through with. Did he or she follow the agenda they planned on? What unexpected obstacles got in their way? How has the public's opinion of them changed since they got elected?

The Evening Star

LANDSLIDE!
Gluck Wins!

Candidat
erbes in BX..

Take a Stand! Crossword Puzzle

DOWN

1. He or she represents your state in Congress.
2. The president's way of saying "NO" to Congress.
3. A law in the making.
4. Local political activity.
5. The World Court is located in the _____ Nations.
6. Our Constitution says that all people are created this way.
7. The day the Supreme Court gives their Opinions.
8. National Aeronautics and Space Administration.
9. Talk all day for a fili_____.
10. They cast the final vote for president.

ACROSS

A. Person who helps for free.
B. Candidates arguing.
C. Government by the people.
D. Adding laws to the Constitution.
E. The Court whose decision is final.
F. *I Like Ike,* and other sayings.
G. All plants and animals live in an eco_____.
H. The Tuesday after the first Monday in November every four years.
I. A natural resource that cannot be recycled.
J. A document that ends disagreements.

(Answers on page 64)

How to Win a School + Election

Deciding to run for school office is a big decision!

You'll have to commit lots of time to running a campaign and you might not win, even if you are the best person for the job! You might have to run in several campaigns before you get elected; however, whether or not you ultimately become a student official, running for office is a good experience that will teach you what it's like to be a public figure!

Many politicians started by getting involved at school. You may have dreamed of being a senator or even a president someday. School offices are a good way of learning the basics about what politicians do and what they go through.

What are your odds?

Different schools have different governments with different offices. Often, they have a student body president, a vice president, a treasurer, a secretary, an events organizer, and assorted members and representatives. In many schools, you need to participate in student government for a year or more before you can run for the presidency.

In addition, different schools have different election periods. Some schools hold one election in the fall, while others hold an election each semester. In some schools, you will need to be nominated. Some schools even require that you get the approval of one or more teachers before you run for office. You may even have to get a petition signed by a number of students to be nominated.

Many people treat school elections as if they were a popularity contest. These people may make a big splash before they get elected but they aren't likely to follow through on the promises they make. Don't run for office just to see how many of your friends will vote for you. If you win, you'll end up with a lot of responsibilities you don't really want!

Are you ready for the commitment?

Being a student body official takes time and patience. Most schools require that you maintain a decent grade point average in order to run for office. That means a full homework schedule along with lots of new responsibilities, including after-school meetings, agendas, minutes, event organization, and assemblies. You will probably have lots of trouble if you intend to run for a major office and you want to be involved in a sport, drama, or other club that requires a lot of your time.

Organizing a team

Every good election campaign needs a good campaign manager.

Ask a close friend to be your **campaign manager,** somebody you can trust, who is a hard worker with a lot of good ideas. Your campaign manager will have to help you develop a platform, write speeches, promote your name around school, and nab those votes!

A good campaign manager has to be dedicated and willing to work hard. In return, you need to respect their schedule, their opinion, and their plan for helping you win. If your school allows you to, you should appoint them to a position, such as vice president or council member of the student body, should you win the election.

Fill the Void: Finding Out the Needs of Your People.

A good politician understands who he or she is representing—what they want done and why. The people a politician represents are known as his or her **constituents**.

The best way to find out what your constituents want is to ask around campus. You may even want to give people a survey with different questions for them to answer.

- What are their daily concerns?
- What makes them angry?
- What changes would they like to see made on campus?
- Do they like the cafeteria food?
- Can a new way of doing things be introduced?
- Are there clubs or organizations they would like to form?
- Are there events, parades, or dances that your peers would like to see take place?

You and your campaign manager need to petition your fellow students at lunch and find out what they care about. Gather your survey results and make a list from most common to least common concerns. The most common concerns are the ones you will want to address for your platform.

For instance, let's say that four students remarked that the school needed recycling bins, twelve students complained about the bad cafeteria food, and thirty-two students claimed that what they wanted most was a noon-time dance on campus. Noon-time dances would become your most common concern, and the most important one to address in your speeches and your campaign.

How to Write (and Deliver) Speeches That'll Knock Their Socks Off.

A good speech is the single most important tool for winning your election. Through a good speech your student body can get to know you. You may speak in front of the whole assembly, or you may be asked to speak in front of several classes.

Stage Fright: The Universal Fear

Statistics show that stage fright is the number one fear in the Western world ... worse than the fear of death! So don't feel bad if you've been getting pre-speech jitters. It's only natural. When we speak in public our mouths dry up, our hearts start pounding, our knees tremble, we feel dizzy and disoriented, and we sweat buckets.

Why do we get stage fright and how can we ever overcome it? Stage fright is nothing more than our natural reaction to facing a crowd as a single individual. It feels like every pair of eyes on the planet is staring straight at us! Our worst fears are really silly when you think about it:

- I have nothing to say.
- People are going to laugh at me or think I'm a fool.
- Some crazy thing will happen and everything will go wrong.

The good news is that anyone can overcome stage fright. There are two simple steps to being able to face the crowd and win them over: *preparation* and *conversation*.

Preparation:

A good speech is well-organized. A good speaker is like a tour guide, taking the audience on a journey of his or her thoughts and ideas.

Most great election speeches start with a humorous or moving **introduction**, then quickly state the speaker's **purpose.** The purpose is backed up by **examples** and the examples are solved by a **solution** or solutions. Finally, the speaker sums it all up with a **conclusion.**

Introduction:

Start your speech with a short, funny story that relates to your purpose. By opening with something lighthearted, people will listen to you more carefully. Has something happened to you recently that might tie in to what you are going to talk about?

Purpose:

The single most important piece of preparation you'll need to do is decide what the purpose of your speech is. In this case, it's easy. You are running for student office. Your job is to answer the audience's imaginary question:

Why should we elect you?

Examples:

Here, you take the information you discovered in the chapter titled *Fill the Void: Finding Out the Needs of Your People* and apply it to your speech! Take all those issues and problems your fellow students told you about and throw it back at them! Let them know that you have heard their ideas and complaints, and that you understand them.

Start with the most insignificant examples and build, until you are speaking about the most important. You may not have too much time, so you'll want to talk about the issues people care about the most.

Most importantly, let them know what you plan to do to make things better. Just like the president of the United States, let them know your agenda of *solutions*.

There's More

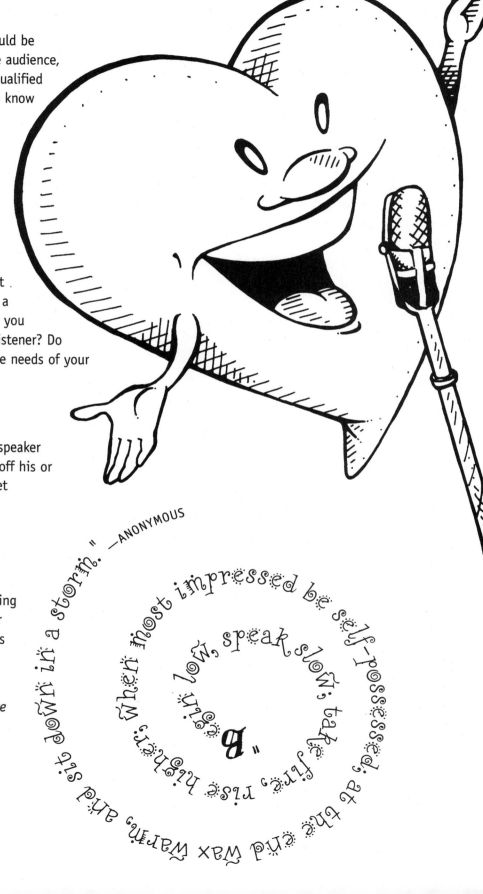

Solutions:

Now that you've identified what should be done at your school, how do we, the audience, know that you are the person best qualified to take care of business? How do we know that you have the solutions?

- What have you done in the past that makes you a good leader?
- Have you had any experience volunteering or leading a school group?
  - What are your best qualities? Are you a good student? Are you friendly? A good listener? Do you understand the needs of your fellow classmates?

Conclusion:

Have you ever seen a speaker that just couldn't shut off his or her mouth-faucet and get off the stage?

You must conclude your speech quickly and simply so that people remember you instead of trying to forget you! Your basic final message is obvious:

I am _____ .

I will be a great representative who will take care of your needs.

Vote for me.

"Be self-possessed at the end and sit down in a storm." —ANONYMOUS

"Begin low, speak slow, take fire, rise higher; when most impressed be self-possessed; at the end wax warm, and sit down in a storm." —ANONYMOUS

Conversation: Know Your Speech by Heartfelt Heart

To truly know your speech by heart takes more than memorization—it takes understanding. You should be familiar enough with the words so that you are comfortable talking rather than reciting. What if (oh no!) somebody interrupts you with a question? Are you relaxed enough with your material so that you can pause, answer them, and continue? Or will you break out in a cold sweat and freeze like a statue!? If you know your speech by heart, it will become like conversation to you.

The best speakers don't just navigate their audience with words. They also convey emotion. When you address a problem at school that's been bugging everyone, let them know that it bugs you too! Show them that you really care, that you're committed to making changes. When you truly understand your speech and can convey the emotion behind the words, your audience will care too!

The only way to really know a speech with complete confidence is to practice, practice, practice. Deliver it for family and friends before you face the classrooms. Go over it with your campaign manager and supporters. Let them help you write and rewrite it. After all, it's their needs that you are representing.

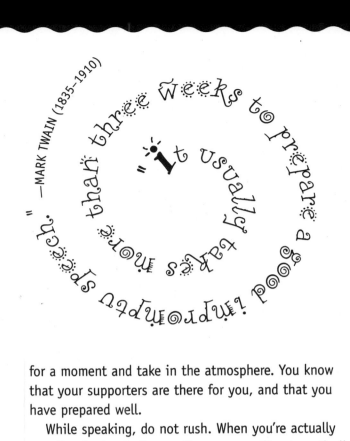

"It usually takes more than three weeks to prepare a good impromptu speech." —MARK TWAIN (1835–1910)

Delivering the Speech

When the time comes to finally give your speech, stretch and take a few deep breaths to clear your mind and relax your body. Make sure that you are dressed comfortably. Drink a glass of water beforehand to quench your thirst.

Approach the podium with confidence. Your fellow students will be "sizing you up" from the moment you take the stage. Don't run but don't dilly-dally either! Look out at the audience for a moment and take in the atmosphere. You know that your supporters are there for you, and that you have prepared well.

While speaking, do not rush. When you're actually standing in front of an audience, you will automatically try to talk faster, no matter how confident you feel. Take your time and enunciate, pacing yourself for the full stretch of the speech. Don't worry about how the audience reacts. If they don't laugh at your introduction, do not panic. They may be listening very intently, but you'll never know because you can't read their minds. Your job is to say what you have to say in a clear and understandable way.

When you are done, smile and step away from the podium calmly. You've stated your case well. Perhaps you've won some new people over. You won't know for sure until election day!

The Great Debate

If your school holds debates for school office candidates, be sure that you are prepared! Know the possible questions that might come up ahead of time and prepare short easy-to-understand answers.

Here are a few helpful hints for debating:

- Never attack the other candidates personally. This only makes you look like a fool who doesn't have solutions of your own.

- Always make sure your promises and solutions are realistic. Your fellow students will know if they're being given a snow job!

- Be clear about how you will answer questions, no matter how your audience reacts. Nobody likes a candidate who changes his or her mind just to catch up with popular opinion!

For more help, read *How to Hold a Mock Election* (pp. 43–46) and *How to Deliver Speeches* (pp. 50–53).

True Heroics Versus Smear Campaigns

A smear campaign attempts to uncover an opponent's bad behavior. Often, when the public finds out that a candidate has been suspected of cheating, lying, stealing, or some other bad behavior, they decide that he or she is not trustworthy enough to hold a public office.

Smear campaigns are not very cool because they don't center on what's good about you. They focus on what's bad about the other guy. Just because he or she isn't trustworthy doesn't mean that you are a good candidate. Try to win your election by focusing on your strengths, not others' weaknesses. That way, if you win, you'll win because the people really want you!

"Preparation is the key to victory." —WINSTON CHURCHILL

The Fine Art of Promotion

A great campaign needs to capture everybody's attention and make them really want to elect you candidate. For this, you need promotion—also known as encouragement through advertising. There are several great ways to promote a candidate, including slogans, buttons, posters, fliers, announcements, and events.

Adopt a Slogan

The best presidential campaigns have all had quick, easy-to-read and easy-to-remember slogans plastered on posters and buttons:

> All the Way with LBJ
> I Like Ike
> Nixon's the One

Your campaign needs a slogan that people will see in a flash and remember all the way to the ballot box! Is there a platform you are running on that can easily be summarized next to your name?

Here are some examples to get you going:

- *Mary Sims for Student Body President: Better Cafeteria Food and School Recycling!*
- *Tony Thompson for School Treasurer: He Puts His Money Where His Mouth Is!*
- *For a Better Semester Cast Your Vote for Dawn Olivas for 10th Grade President!*

In 1964, Barry Goldwater ran under the slogan, "In Your Heart You Know He's Right." His opposition counterattacked with the saying, "In Your Guts You Know He's Nuts."

Posters

When it comes to posters, the bigger and brighter and simpler the better! Try creating a poster that people can read while rushing to class, with a simple slogan and a simple image they'll remember. If you've created a slogan, make sure the poster includes it.

Buttons

Today, most party stores have blank buttons on which you can draw your slogan and pass out to students. A bright button on somebody's backpack is a good way to help them to remember your name! Tags with strings or with safety pins also work just fine.

Announcements

Ask your principal or guidance counselor if you can make a brief 30 second announcement over the school intercom. To be fair, all the other candidates must get the same time.

You can have your campaign manager read an advertisement such as the following: "This week, when you cast your vote for student body president, be sure to remember Mary Sims, the candidate for better food and an official school recycling program. Mary Sims—she cares about you!"

Or perhaps you can try reading an announcement yourself, such as: "Hi, this is Mary Sims, candidate for student body president. I just want everyone to know that if I'm elected, I promise to keep my commitment to better school food and an official recycling program. So this week, when you cast your ballot, vote for me—Mary Sims for student body president."

Caution!
Follow School Rules!

Not all schools allow fliers, posters, rallies, buttons, and balloons during school elections. Be sure to ask a teacher, guidance counselor, or principal if your campaign follows school procedure. You'll never get elected if you get suspended for breaking the rules!

The Big Rally

At least once before the big election day, you'll want to hold a rally just like presidential candidates do. Get your supporters to gather with posters and balloons and noisemakers. When you've got them all in one place, have your campaign manager formally introduce you and make a short speech, explaining your platform and letting your fans know that they are making the right choice by supporting you. Lunch-time onlookers are sure to notice and perhaps even participate in the rally!

Press Tent

You may want to set up a regular place on campus during lunch where you will be available for any questions. As a candidate, it's essential for you to be as available as possible before election day. You may convince a handful of people to vote for you and end up winning because of their support! At many schools, it only takes one vote to break a tie!

Campaign Plan Checklist

Have you remembered to:

✔ Make sure that you can commit to running for office?

✔ Find out the needs of your fellow students?

✔ Create a platform that addresses their needs?

✔ Prepare and practice a speech that lets them know you're the best person for the job?

✔ Create a simple slogan to help people to remember you and your platform?

✔ Promote yourself through posters, buttons, fliers, announcements, rallies, and a press tent?

If the answer is yes to all of these questions, then you are definitely ready to run! Good luck!

FREDDIE IS READY!

Now That You've Won: Good Leadership

Promises, Promises

Now that you've won, your battle really begins! You've got to complete the task at hand: making good on all those promises that got you elected in the first place. Remember the most basic principle of modern democracy: The best leaders serve the needs of the people they represent.

As an elected official of the student body, you represent your fellow students to the parents, teachers, administration, and principal of your school. If you don't take your job seriously, adults might not take your fellow students seriously. However, if you excel as a representative, adults will respect your peers, and your peers will love you for it!

Delegation and Teamwork

As strange as it seems, the best leaders know when to stop leading and start **delegating** their power to others! Just as you had a campaign manager to help you achieve student office, you'll need the hard work of a lot of people to keep your student body happy.

As a student official, you're sure to have many great experiences that will teach you how to make changes, and help improve your school and the world around you. Remember that you're carrying the torch for our great nation and our great tradition of democracy—government by the people!

Do's and Don'ts for the Rookie Leader

Always...

1. Listen to your fellow students
2. Choose your battles
3. Remember your platform or agenda

Never...

1. Act like a hot shot
2. Take it personally
3. Forget the basic principle of democracy: freedom (yours *and* others')

"Kings are the proprietors of the people, not the servants." —THOMAS JEFFERSON, 1774

Government on the Internet

Now you can access government information, write officials, and even e-mail the president when you cybersurf the Internet. The following are a few government-related hot spots that are jam-packed with information and activities:

- **THOMAS**

  Located on the World Wide Web at http://thomas.loc.gov, THOMAS is the White House home page, featuring information on bills in Congress, a welcome message from the president, and a tour of the White House grounds.

- **LOCIS**

  This is the telnet site for the Library of Congress, featuring information on bills and laws dating back to 1973. LOCIS is located at locis.loc.gov, and features a special section where you can e-mail members of the House of Representatives and read their daily floor speeches and press releases.

- **GOVERNMENT AGENCIES at**
  http://www.lib.lsu.edu/gov/fedgov/html

  This superlong address is the key to the World Wide Web Virtual Library's U.S. Government Agencies section. If there is a department of government in the United States that you want to learn more about, this is the place to start!

- **GOVERNMENT DOCUMENTS:**
  ftp.spies.com and nova.cc.purdue.edu

  These FTP libraries contains famous speeches, inaugural addresses, laws, and documents that date as far back as the Mayflower Compact, Washington's Farewell Address, and the Magna Carta. Great inspiration for when you're planning to make your great speech!

- **UNITED NATIONS**

  Located on the World Wide Web at http://www.undp.org, the United Nations features access to the world through it's most central institution!

Here are some other fun Internet addresses where you can find out about government news, information, and activities:

USENET.NEWS
alt.politics.media
alt.politics.usa.constitution
alt.politics.usa.misc
soc.politics

TELNET
fedworld.gov
fedix.fie.com

FTP
ftp.senate.gov/committee
ftp.loc.gov/pub/reference.guides/us.govt.

GOPHER
gopher.census.gov
gopher.house.gov
gopher.senate.gov

WORLD WIDE WEB
http://lcweb.loc.gov
http://fedworld.gov
http://www.whitehouse.gov
http://yahoo.com/Government

Agenda
A program of tasks or goals to be accomplished.

Amendment
A change or addition to an existing law.

Anonymous
Having an unknown name, no revealed identity.

Articles of Confederation
In 1787 Congress endorsed this document that called for no central government. That same year, the states revised this to create the U.S. Constitution.

Ballot box
Secured container that holds voting cards.

Bill
A proposed law.

Bill of Rights
The first ten amendments in the Constitution.

Cabinet
The group of officials who advise the U.S. president.

Campaign manager
Someone who helps you organize an election campaign.

Candidate committee
The group who researches the views of student presidential candidates.

Capital
A town or city that is the official seat of government in a state or nation.

Capitol
A building where legislature meets, such as the White House in Washington D.C.

Checks & balances
A system by which the three branches of government (legislative, executive, and judicial) watch over each other, so the needs of the people are best represented, and no one branch gains too much power.

City council
The governing body of a city.

City hall
Building where mayor has an office.

Conclusion
The end of your speech where you summarize your purpose, examples, and solution.

Conference committee
The group that resolves the differences between versions of bills submitted by the House and the Senate.

Congress
Council made up of senators and representatives sent to Washington D.C. from each state.

Constituents
The people an elected official represents.

Constitutional Convention.
Meeting in 1787 at which our forebears planned our government.

Constitution of the United States
Adopted by all the states in 1790, this document establishes the Bill of Rights and the laws of our nation.

Continental Congress
Congress for the American colonies.

Debate committee
The group who decides what questions to ask a candidate in a debate.

Declaration of Independence
The document that established America's independence from England.

Delegate
To share your power or responsibility to complete a task or make decisions.

Democracy
Government by the people.

Diplomat
Official who is trained in dealing tactfully with other countries.

Economic and Social Council
Coordinates the economic and social work of the United Nations, and its agencies.

Ecosystem
The balance between a group of living creatures and their environment.

Election day
The Tuesday after the first Monday in November. The presidential election is held once every four years. Elections for representatives and for some senators (one-third of the Senate) are held once every two years.

Elector
A member of the electoral college who represents the voters in his or her state.

Electoral college
Total number of senators and representatives who vote for the individual states.

Equal
Having the same privileges, status, or rights as someone else.

Examples
Facts or comparisons that support your purpose.

Executive branch
The president, the president's office, and the president's cabinet, responsible for executing U.S. laws and administration.

Federal government
Makes decisions that affect *all* U.S. citizens.

Filibuster
This debate tactic, where a senator talks endlessly to wear down his or her opponents, was made famous in the movie, *Mr. Smith Goes to Washington*.

Founding Forefathers
The people who helped start our nation, including George Washington, Benjamin Franklin, James Madison, and Alexander Hamilton.

Freedom
The capacity to exercise free will; liberty from slavery and oppression.

General Assembly
Department of the UN that discusses important world problems.

Governor
The head of government for each state, who works in the state capitol.

Grassroots
Community-level activism.

House of Representatives
This part of the legislative branch is made up of 435 representatives from all 50 states.

Individual
A person with special qualities distinguished from others; a human being.

International Court of Justice (World Court)
Settles legal disputes between countries.

Introduction
The beginning of your speech where you introduce yourself and state your purpose.

Judicial branch
Handles administration of justice, includes the Supreme Court.

Judicial review
Process by which the Supreme Court reviews laws and treaties.

Legislation
Proposed or enacted laws.

Legislative branch (Congress)
Studies, and enacts laws and rules; includes the Senate and the House of Representatives.

Legislative counsel
Reviews bills to ensure that they are legal and constitutional.

Local government
Manages police and fire departments, libraries, local courts, and transportation.

Mayor
The head of government of a city, who works from city hall.

Mock election
A student body presidential campaign that will teach you about "real life" politics.

NASA
National Aeronautics Space Administration. Organization that governs space.

Purpose
The main thought in your speech, probably about what you will accomplish as student body leader.

Rebut
To offer an opposing argument during a debate.

Recycling
Processing used aluminum, glass, paper, plastic, and other items into reusable raw materials.

Representative
Member of the group of people who help run the legislative branch. The number of representatives from each state varies according to its population. Representatives are given two-year terms. Representative *also* describes the kind of democracy the U.S. has, where elected officials *represent* our interests and needs.

Secretariat
The staff that handles the daily affairs at the United Nations.

Security Council
Department of the United Nations that is concerned with peace and security.

Senate
This part of the legislative branch is made up of one hundred senators from each state.

Senators
Member of the group of people who help run the legislative branch. Two senators from each state are given a six-year term.

Separation of powers
A system by which the three branches of government (executive, legislative, and judicial) all handle different functions.

Solution
Your ideas for how to solve the problems facing the student body.

Sponsor
Any member of Congress who supports a particular bill.

State capitol
Building where state affairs are managed, and where the governor has an office.

State government
Handles education, public safety, recreation, welfare, and conservation.

Supreme Court
The highest federal court in the U.S.

Treaty
An agreement between two countries regarding terms of peace and trade.

Trusteeship Council
Promotes self-government for territories.

United Nations
Worldwide organization that promotes world peace and communication.

Veto
When a president exercises his or her power to refuse to sign a bill to make it a law.

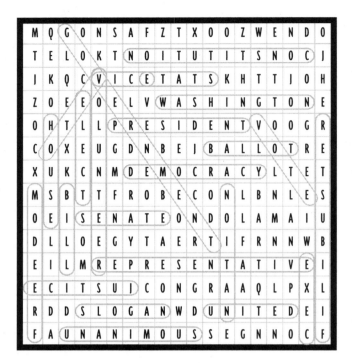

M	Q	G	O	N	S	A	F	Z	T	X	O	O	Z	W	E	N	D	O
T	E	L	O	K	T	N	O	I	T	U	T	I	T	S	N	O	C	J
I	K	Q	C	V	I	C	E	T	A	T	S	K	H	T	T	J	O	H
Z	O	E	E	O	E	L	V	W	A	S	H	I	N	G	T	O	N	E
O	H	T	L	L	P	R	E	S	I	D	E	N	T	V	O	O	G	R
C	O	X	E	U	G	D	N	B	E	J	B	A	L	L	O	T	R	E
X	U	K	C	N	M	D	E	M	O	C	R	A	C	Y	L	T	E	T
M	S	B	T	T	F	R	O	B	E	C	O	N	L	B	N	L	E	S
O	E	I	S	E	N	A	T	E	O	N	D	O	L	A	M	A	I	U
D	L	L	O	E	G	Y	T	A	E	R	T	I	F	R	N	N	W	B
E	I	L	M	R	E	P	R	E	S	E	N	T	A	T	I	V	E	I
E	C	I	T	S	U	J	C	O	N	G	R	A	A	Q	L	P	X	L
R	D	D	S	L	O	G	A	N	W	D	U	N	I	T	E	D	E	I
F	A	U	N	A	N	I	M	O	U	S	S	E	G	N	N	O	C	F

Match the Anti People!

F	**1.**	Antinomians
J	**2.**	Antifederalists
G	**3.**	Antimasons
D	**4.**	Anti-Imperialist League
I	**5.**	Antimonopoly Party
A	**6.**	Antibigamy Act
B	**7.**	Antitrust Movement
K	**8.**	Antisaloon League of America
C	**9.**	Anti-Injunction Act
E	**10.**	Anti-Anticommunism
H	**11.**	Antiballistic Missile Treaty

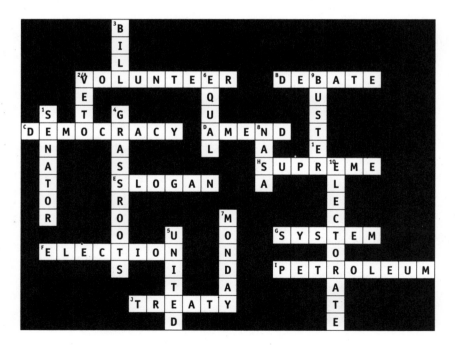